AKWA

& THE SEA GODDESS

First Journey

ALLY THOMAS

Illustrations by Ally Thomas

Akwa and the Sea Goddess: First Journey © Ally Thomas 2023

www.allythomas.com.au/author

www.allythomas.com.au/artist

The moral rights of Ally Thomas to be identified as the author of this work have been asserted in accordance with the Copyright Act 1968.

Edited by Dominic Gilmour

Cover design and map by SusansArt.

First published in Australia 2022 by Opalise Publishing

ISBN 978-0-9946228-4-6

Any opinions expressed in this work are exclusively those of the author and are not necessarily the views held or endorsed by the Publisher.

Adelaide SA Australia

Dedicated to all the sea lovers,
and to all the Goddesses
with gratitude

Table of Contents

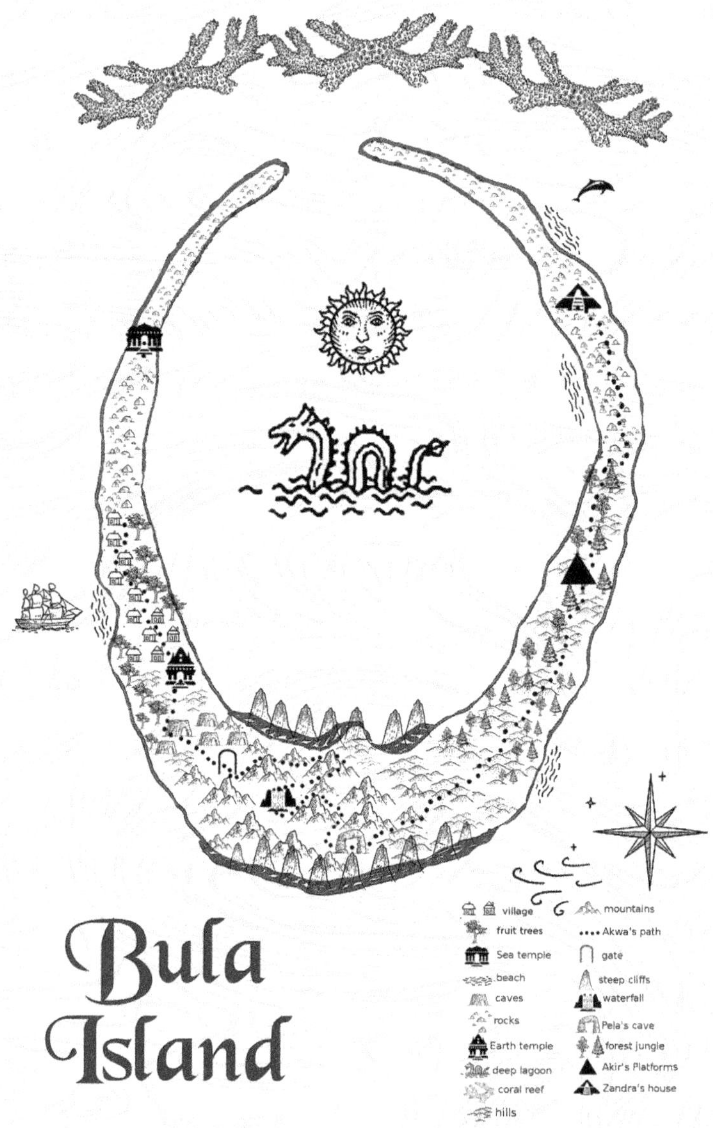

Figure 1: Map of Bula Island

Prologue

"Home is where your heart is."

"There's no such thing as a Red Dragon Troll!" said Kiwi, shaking her head emphatically.

"Oh, yes there is!" said Akwa, just as strongly.

"You're being stupid! We'd know if they were real."

"My mum says so," Akwa replied to her best friend.

"She's just a good storyteller, a dream weaver. It's not *really* true. Have you ever seen one?" Kiwi retorted. "How big are they? How do they spin their webs? Why do they like to eat fingers and toes? Which streams do they live in? How do they tempt their victims?"

Akwa had no reply. No answers.

All the people in her village on Bula Island had heard the stories that Akwa's mother, Moana, told. They were based on ancient tales, passed from mother to daughter in the Bard family. But to Akwa, they were more than stories. She knew they were true, as real as the history of the island itself.

"They must be based on something that really happened long ago. Otherwise, how could they be made up?" she mused.

"Prove it then," Kiwi dared. "Prove that they're real."

Akwa opened her mouth to argue, paused, then shut it again. Kiwi rolled her eyes.

"I thought so."

Chapter 1
Akwa

Introducing Akwa and Bula Island

Akwa lived happily with her mother Moana and father Tahi in a small village on the tropical, crescent-shaped Bula Island in the vast, blue ocean.

Bula Island was surrounded by a huge coral reef, and the village was on the western side. There was a Sea Temple dedicated to the sea goddess close to the north-western tip and a calm lagoon lapped in the middle of the island, though its depths were rumoured to be treacherous, so the villagers neither swam nor paddled there.

The men of the village were fishermen, and the woman grew food – they planted taro roots and tended their tropical fruit trees in a plantation on the sheltered inner-western side of the island. They lived in peaceful harmony with the land and the sea, respecting the power of the elements.

In the southern middle area of the island were steep, foreboding mountains, with sheer cliffs plunging deep into the sea on either side. They divided the island in half, and stories of the trolls and monsters that lived in the streams and rocky places abounded. Most of the villagers were too scared to navigate the trails that led to their peaks, so they had never been to the Mountain Temple in the middle of the mountains, never venturing past the stone arch Gateway.

It was said that people with strange customs lived on the other side of the mountain. They were said to communicate with the animals who lived there – bears and tigers and other beasts – and they held ritualistic ceremonies which involved feasting, dancing and intimacy with spirits and gods.

There were also stories about a mad old crone – some stories said she was a wise woman – who used to live in Akwa's village. She had magic energy, and it was rumoured that she could talk to the sea birds. Other stories told of her turning people into monkeys and lizards. The tales that were whispered around campfires told that she was banished from the village because of her magic, forced into the mountains and told to never come back.

There was always debate, though. Did she just decide to go and live on the other side of the island, or was she banished? Was she still alive? What was the truth?

Akwa

Akwa had jet black curly hair, unlike most of the other people in her village, who had long, straight dark hair and dark brown eyes. Her eyes were light turquoise, like the colour of the lagoon, but when she was deep in thought, her eyes became the ultramarine blue of the ocean far from land. She was bubbly and happy, with healing hands. And sometimes, her dreams came true.

Not only did Akwa stand out from others in the village because she looked different, but things happened around her which she couldn't explain.

Once, when she was younger, Akwa and her friends were playing on the beach when she saw a dolphin drifting toward them, three others seemingly holding it up in the water. It was unusual for dolphins to come through the outer coral reef and into the lagoon, and unheard of for the creatures to approach the islanders.

Akwa immediately waded into the water, despite the calls and cries from her friends. She stood still in the waist-deep water and slowly reached out her hand. The dolphin gently floated towards her, guided by its support pod. Instead of the comforting noises the other dolphins made, this one's were weak, very quiet. In her heart, Akwa felt the distress of the dolphin as jagged, rough, black feelings. So she imagined clear, blue, wavy feelings flowing from her heart down into the dolphin's.

After a while the dolphin became more buoyant, and its clicks and whistles changed, growing louder, rising and falling with energy. The trio of dolphins also changed their comforting whistle sounds. Eventually the healed dolphin pulled away and swam with its pod northwards to the opening of the lagoon, toward the outer reef. Akwa watched as they swam away, and as they reached the mouth of the lagoon, the four dolphins somersaulted for their audience.

One day, when she was fifteen years old, Moana told Akwa about her beginnings. Although

Tahi and Moana had tried many times, Moana couldn't have a baby, so she had prayed to Sedna the Sea Goddess at the Sea Temple. It was midnight, on a full moon night, and with her back to the stars and moon reflecting in the ocean, she knelt and fervently prayed.

The next day, Tahi found a baby in a little boat on the beach. Moana expressed her joy and happiness when he bought Akwa home. Their dreams had come true! Akwa, their own child to love, cherish and teach. A special blessing – a gift from the sea goddess!

***

Sea traders from all over the world came and visited the island, though their visits were rare. They brought exotic items from faraway places. Some stayed because the island and its women were very beautiful. Sometimes Akwa would try to communicate with the traders and find out where they came from, learning all about their islands and their ways of life.

She was curious about all things and enjoyed learning about other tribes, different customs, and people's lives. Sometimes they indulged her, but sometimes she didn't understand what they were talking about as their language was foreign to her, and they only spoke her Bula Island language roughly, with mispronounced words and strange expressions.

Moana

Moana, Akwa's mother, had a shapely figure, long, straight dark hair and full breasts. Akwa thought she was the most beautiful woman in the village. She was always happy and nurturing to the women and girls.

Moana was the Bula Island bard and loved to tell stories. She would entertain the village with stories of ancient wisdom, telling tales of Sedna the Sea Goddess, Gaia the Earth Goddess, Pela the Mountain Goddess, the cheeky monkeys, red dragon trolls and the wise woman, Zandra.

She also regaled the youngsters with traditional stories about the three temples and goddesses of sea, land and mountain. She taught them the rituals associated with worshipping the goddesses and giving thanks.

The stories that fascinated Akwa most were about the history of the ancient caves in the hills where the island folk went for healing, meditation, rituals and shelter. And in some of the caves, there were symbols – ancient runes carved by the unknown ancestors of Bula Island. There were many prophetic stories about the Ultimate Rune signs that Moana told as well, and the village always gathered to listen whenever she had a story to share, even if they'd heard it before.

Tahi

Akwa's father, Tahi, was popular in the village. He was a tall, happy, well-built man, and always had a smile for everyone. His hair was short and dark-chocolate brown. He was always well groomed and looked and smelled clean. Akwa loved everything about him, and adored his gentle, enveloping hugs best of all.

He was a good boat builder and rallied the men together, often inspiring and leading them with his humour, knowledge and wisdom. Tahi also had anecdotes and humorous stories which he passed on to his younger students to help them learn.

Akwa sometimes listened to his words and wished she could be a boy so she could go out in the boats fishing as well. It sounded like a wonderful adventure to her!

Every day the fishermen went fishing – some in the early morning before dawn, and some after nightfall. Frequently, Tahi brought home the most fish, and he shared them with the families who didn't catch enough.

At night, Akwa watched the comforting lights of her dad's fishing boat and the other fishermen's twinkling far across the sea.

Often, in the mornings, she would run down to the beach to see the fish they had caught and welcome the fishermen home. Sometimes there were unusual fish and coloured shells in the nets, which would be studied and sometimes dried to decorate the village as ornaments.

The Caves of the Ancients

The Caves of the Ancients were deep caverns in the lower foothills on the south-western side of the island. Their maze-like tunnels joined to form a network of linked caverns, some of which burrowed deep underground. No one knew if they were natural or carved out by the ancestors of the inhabitants of Bula Island, but they were huge, echoing chambers which the village had come to use for storage and shelter when the seas were rough and stormy.

If the villagers walked far enough, exploring into the very heart of the mountains, they'd eventually come to the Royal Caves. These were used for special ceremonies, and only the elders knew how to reach them without getting lost. It was rumoured that they held meetings and initiations in the deepest of the Royal Caves, and their location was a closely guarded secret among the elders.

The caverns closer to the surface had enough space for the whole village to live in comfortably during times of emergency, which acted as a safe haven because they were above the highest known sea level.

Drawn on the walls of many of the caves were runic symbols. No one knew who carved them, or even what they meant, but every child on Bula Island knew the traditional stories about the runes and prophecies. They believed that they were all just stories which had been handed down in Moana's family for generations and told to children and adults for entertainment.

Moana had a scroll on which she had copied the most repeated runes. These same runes were also repeated in a big carved version on the main wall of one of the Royal Caves, and the scroll had been given to Moana as a gift. (See 'The Scroll of Ancient Runes and their Meanings' on page 124).

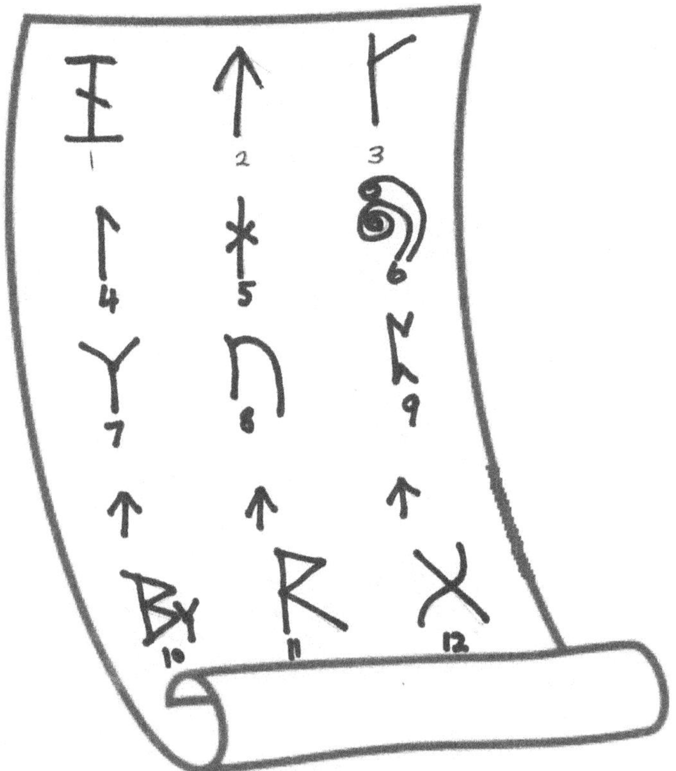

Figure 2: Moana's scroll of the Runes

Over the years, many people had speculated about the meanings of these runes, and of the prophecies of the three Ultimate Rune Signs. These were drawn and carved in several of the caves in different ways. Some of the villagers had their own interpretations of what the runes and prophecies could mean, and during a mid-summer full moon celebration when Akwa was a girl, the village discussed their interpretations.

It was late into the night, the sun finally set. They had created a great fire on the beach and danced under the light of the moon. It was part of an ancient all-night full moon ritual and they'd be there until the sun rose. Taking a break from dancing with her friends, Akwa had sought her mum and listened, fascinated, as the village discussed their interpretations. She couldn't remember all of what everyone said, but Kiwi's mum was first.

She stood up when she spoke, sharing her beliefs in earnest. "They tell us of survival, that we need a strong male leader, like my husband, to keep the boats and village safe. The runes say that together we can control the natural forces of the world. We can control our boats on the sea and survive the storms. We navigate using the stars and the currents, we can look to the skies and predict whether there will be sun or rain. The world is a tool for us to use so we can thrive, but the only way we can do that is with a generous ruler to give his powerful love to all his family and village. After all, with strong leadership, we can weather any storm.

"Sometimes love and leadership decisions are hidden and need to be explained afterwards. Anger can be forgiven – we all make mistakes, so we can all live without blame. The ancestors have left it clearly for us in the runes: women are to obey, nurture and support, and we all look our leader for a good life. The gods will give us gifts through our strong male leader."

Kiwi's mum sat down again to murmurs of approval and hushed discussion. Akwa wasn't sure what to think. *Am I really just here to obey and support others? We need a strong leader, but there's more to my life, isn't there? What about love?*

After some discussion of those ideas, Kriti's dad gave the masculine viewpoint. "The runes are about distress, and we need male authority to manage it – to build bigger boats to protect and control the unpredictable female emotions of creation and destruction. Our brave fishermen go out in all weathers.

The sea is strong, but we ride through it, and after the storm, we go fishing again. My philosophy is that life is a game, and we are the winners; mistakes are to be learned from, and women are to be loved, honoured and respected. Men control the journey of life, we are god-like and give gifts to women."

This time, before Kriti's dad could sit down again, there were outbursts of disagreement, though Akwa thought the two theories were quite similar. She didn't say anything, but neither of these felt true to her.

Just as arguments were starting to break out, Uluru's mum rose to her feet, silencing the group. She was very spiritual, a gentle and frail woman, and greatly respected among the village. She spoke softly, the sound of waves washing ashore behind her. "It is only with grace and by honouring the partnership of male and female that we can all flow with life on a calm ocean. Dreams become real if we pray to the sea goddess. We pray to calm our emotions and ride the waves of life. Nature is a wonderful, powerful creator. We are eternal. We reincarnate to be born again. When we are initiated, we are connected with a spiritual abundance of love, so we must remember our connection to the rainbow serpent which will always return with joy, happiness and love.

The world is not for us to wrangle to our own will, but rather we must follow where it takes us, letting it show us the way to better times and a better way of life. Our matriarchal customs support us, and we learn and grow on our spiritual journey of life with messages from spirit guides and goddesses."

A sombre silence settled over the group as they absorbed her words. Akwa couldn't remember any other theories from that night, but Moana's personal interpretation of the runes was simple: she read it like a story. A man is lost at sea. The Sea Goddess is angry; she sends gigantic waves, a storm, destruction.

Fruit survives on trees for people to eat, and as life changes, everyone must be open to changing their interpretation and beliefs. A woman with gifts goes on a journey to consult the ancient wise crone, though she is not alone. She has guidance, help and support from spirit guides, gods and goddesses.

Akwa had heard this uncomplicated interpretation of the runes many times, and

something within her rang true. She wasn't
sure what it was, but something inside her
made her trust her mother's words.

Sedna

Akwa loved the ocean. She loved playing in
the waves or watching a stormy sea, but she
especially loved the quiet moments as the
sun set over the calm, orange sea, the clouds
painted gold, a pathway leading to the sun
splayed across the water.

Every day the villagers had a ritual. First,
they picked a shell from the beach and took
it to the Sea Temple on the north-western tip
of Bula Island. There, they dedicated their
shell offerings to Sedna, the Sea Goddess,
to help protect the fishermen when they
were at sea.

Next, they walked the well-worn path down
the island to the Earth Temple, which was
between the village and the ancient caves.
They took a flower offering, sometimes a

single beautiful hibiscus flower or a posy of blossoms, and dedicated it to Gaia, the Earth Goddess, for an abundant harvest on the land. They did those rituals twice a day, morning and evening, at each of the temples.

Akwa preferred to visit the temples alone, when she could feel it was just her and the sea goddess, so she went to the Sea Temple around midday every day when the sun was highest. It was on the rocky edge of the point of the island, and an inuksuk marked the Sea Temple. On the way, she often collected a special feather or a stone washed smooth by the sea. She prayed for the safety of the fishermen, especially her father. She sang songs that she made up and talked to Sedna. Akwa often felt lulled by the sound of the sea on the shore, as if Sedna whispered to her. When there was stormy surf, Akwa screamed and shouted and sang violent, emotional songs to release her emotions to the sea goddess who listened and roared back.

At the end of each day, Akwa would watch the boats go out, even on wet stormy nights. One night, she could just discern the fishing boats out at sea in a big storm. She could see the lights from their boats ducking and soaring on the waves, getting tossed about and blinking in and out of sight as they fell behind great waves. Akwa kept watch over them, praying to the sea goddess that the fishermen would come home safely. There were so many big waves she couldn't count the lights of all the boats. She began feeling anxious for the fishermen's safety and worried about her father.

Finally, the fishermen came back to the land. Akwa rushed down to meet them on the beach, her intuition warning her that something was wrong. As the fishermen dragged their boats to shore, exhausted and sea-battered, she cried out for her father, called his name, and one of the young fishermen knelt beside her. He looked exhausted, his voice hoarse, and there was heartbreak in his eyes. "Akwa, I'm sorry. He's been taken. Sedna has taken Tahi. He's gone."

Chapter 2

Signs

The Three Signs

They went to find Moana and told her about Tahi. "A big wave came and swept him off his boat. We called him. We searched and searched, but it was too rough to see where he went. We couldn't find his body."

There was much crying and wailing by all the women to express their sorrow and grief. The next night, by moonlight, Akwa went to the Sea Temple and unleashed her emotions. There we so many that she didn't know where to start, and for a time she knelt in the sand and sobbed, the sadness overwhelming her. But then they came, disorderly and uncontrollable.

First of all, fear. Fear of being alone and losing his love. Now that she had lost him, it felt like she had lost him forever. She feared she would never hear his calming voice or his laughter again. She already missed the feeling of his arms around her in his big nurturing hugs. She feared that no one could love her like he did.

Then she felt anger rising. Akwa was angry that the sea goddess had taken him from her. Her anger lashed out in red rage like a whip of pure energy from her fingers to sizzle on the water until disgust swept over her. She was disgusted that this terrible thing could have happened, and for no apparent reason at all. She vented her disapproval to Sedna with wild screams.

And once her throat was raw and her lungs burned, she collapsed on the shore, trembling and exhausted, left with only one emotion remaining. Sadness. Akwa was so sad because she missed her father's happy grin when he teased her and told her whimsical stories.

Akwa ranted and raved at the sea goddess as she tried to release her grief. She felt so lost and betrayed by her idol. She cried salty tears under the cold, silver moon.

The Runes on the Walls of the Caves of the Ancients

Meanwhile, the fishermen searched the sea for Tahi's clothes or body. The women combed the shore, but it was all in vain. Moana, without hope or joy, interpreted the event as the first sign in the ancient runes – *The Lost Man at Sea.*

Figure 3: Runes 1 Nadh (distress, grace, survival), 2 Tyr (man, leadership, honour, authority) and 3 Ka (boat, daring, nothing).

After that, Akwa stopped going to the beach. Every day she prayed. She cajoled and begged

Sedna the Sea Goddess to return her father, and she often had dreams of him being lost and lonely.

The Second Sign

Six months passed. Akwa stopped visiting the Sea Temple and did not sing to the sea goddess. Akwa just trudged around, dejected, living her life in sadness and resignation, lonely and despondent.

One night, Akwa dreamed that Pela, the Mountain Goddess, came to her and told her about a huge volcano that had erupted, and a huge wave was coming. She woke in the middle of the night, afraid. She'd had dreams like this before, and it couldn't wait until morning. She woke Moana, and once a candle was lit and Akwa was safely tucked under the blanket beside her mother, she told Moana about her dream.

By Moana's interpretation of the symbols in the ancient caves, this was the second sign and Akwa's dream confirmed Moana's suspicions – *A Big Wave.* The sea goddess was angry, and she was sending a storm of gigantic waves and destruction.

Figure 4: Runes 4 Logr (sea, water), 5 Hagal (destructive forces), and 6 W (huge waves)

Moana and the elders started to organise the whole village to prepare a retreat to the Caves of the Ancients. They took food, water and precious items with them. Children could choose to assist their mother or father, then they explored the caves. There were large communal caverns for gathering and eating, and smaller tunnels with sleeping pods. Lanterns and glow stones lit the passages and caves in a dim glow, offering just enough light to navigate the tunnels.

Akwa and Moana decorated their caves with seashells and feathers. Kiwi, Akwa's best friend, was close by in her family's cave, and they picked fruit and dug taro and stored the food supplies for the villagers.

The Third Sign

A week later, the winds started blowing and unusual storms came, lasting many days. The people from the village sheltered in the caves. It was even too rough for the fishermen to go out, and as they couldn't bring their boats to the safety of the caves, they lashed them down in the hope of protecting them from the waves. Only people who had to do essential tasks were allowed to venture outside the caves.

A lookout was posted on high ground near the entrance to the caves, and the alarm was raised – the mournful sound of a shell horn – when the water started receding from the land the next day. Everyone sheltered as far back as possible in the caves, and the men built up the sandbag barrier to stop the water coming inside.

They heard and felt a huge tsunami sweep over the island. It crashed over the village and wiped out their wooden houses. The fishing boats were destroyed. All that was left of the village was its people, safely sheltered in the ancient caves.

When the waves subsided and the sea returned to its normal height, the villagers emerged slowly. All the buildings were smashed and uninhabitable. There were broken trees scattered around the remnants

Figure 5: Runes: 7 Kyn (nature, power), 8 Ur (a big storm), 9 Perth (fruit on a tree)

of the village – palm trees, coconut trees, fruit trees. All except one. A big mango tree stood untouched, laden with juicy fruit. The people happily ate the fresh, delicious, ripe mangoes with gratitude.

That, confirmed Moana, was the third and ultimate sign – *The Fruitful Tree*. Moana saw the fruit on the mango tree as a sign that the compassionate and abundant Earth Goddess would provide for all the people.

The men were so devastated that they had lost their precious fishing boats that they disappeared back into the caves and smoked their pipes.

Moana looked at the repeated symbol, a bit like an arrow with a line through it, which meant *wrong* or *mistaken, error, rainbow* and Moana knew what she had to do.

Moana gathered the women for an emergency meeting. Moana told them about the final three runes which gave advice of what to do when the three Ultimate Runes had manifested. She interpreted them as "a woman with gifts goes on a journey to consult the gods and goddesses with help from spirit guides."

Figure 6: Runes 10 Bar (woman birth goddess growth), 11 Radio (journey) and 12 Gibor (gift, giver, gods, spirit guides)

The women decided that they had to take over and organise the clean-up. They talked about the situation at length and agreed that someone would have to go and consult Zandra, the Wise Woman, who they hoped still lived on the other side of the island.

They needed to choose a special woman, the bravest and strongest of the village. But how to decide? After much discussion, argument and brainstorming, they decided to hold a dance competition for all the young women. The winner would be the one to journey across the island to seek help for the community.

Chapter 3
Dance

The Dance Competition

The women announced to the village that a dance competition would be held in seven days to choose a special woman. It would be her honour to seek out the wise woman and ask for her advice. Many preparations were made. To be eligible to enter the competition, the women had to be aged between 15 and 17, not initiated, not married, able to dance well, and have a family to support their entry.

Out of the ten entries, only five were eligible. Each had a team of family helpers – her mother, grandmother and sisters. All helped with choreography, costume design and accessories.

There was much dancing practice. Costumes were designed and made. Curtains, accessories and props were gathered or specially made. As they had just endured the tsunami and lived in the caves for a while, this was a challenging task. Luckily, the resourceful women had taken all their fabrics and sewing implements into the caves for safety. Also, while they were in the caves, they discovered three chests full of richly embroidered costumes, perhaps obtained from the see traders in the past and forgotten about. Some of these were resourcefully adapted and adjusted for their preferred dancers.

The Dancers

On the day of the competition there was great excitement as the whole village gathered at the performance area. The judges sat in front and the villagers sat around them.

Some of the women showed their exotic, off-island heritage with their costume and dances.

Leilani wore a swishy, green skirt made from young coconut fronds. She danced the Tamoure – a love song. Her long hair swayed to the music, her hands telling the story of love and her eyes expressed her heart's desire to give and receive love. The audience fell in love with her. "Aloha!" they crooned.

Kiwi cleverly swung her long *pois* in both hands, moving the flaxen balls attached to lengths of string in graceful arcs, whipping them overhead, while she sang sweetly to her brother's background guitar music. Her words were in the language of her ancestors, but everyone understood their deeply spiritual significance. Her red, white and black *piu piu* flax skirt made a sweet musical sound to accompany her song as she danced.

Uluru's Rainbow Serpent dance told the story of the creation of land, rivers, lakes, water holes and sea. Her rainbow costume glittered and shifted like a snake as her slender body writhed in her earthy dance.

Red-haired Kriti's dance came from a faraway land. The entrancing Grecian siren song was taught to her by her grandmother. Her silvery, metallic dress clung to her body and caught the light in a hypnotic rhythm. By the end, most people were transfixed in a trance.

Finally, to wake them up again, Akwa danced in her turquoise and white sea-watery costume which flowed and frothed like the turquoise waves. In spite of her grief at the loss of her father, and her pain of blaming the sea goddess for taking him from her, she had come to accept these events. So, in her dance, she expressed the story of her joy and love of the sea and Sedna the Sea Goddess – singing and playing, skipping over the sea, swimming and diving deep. She sang of the sea creatures and fish, the storms and calm moods of the sea. And the sea goddess who controlled them all.

Then she expressed her feelings of betrayal and sadness when her father was taken from her. Everyone shed sad tears for Akwa and Sedna the Sea Goddess, as expressed from her song. They were silent when she sank to the ground at the end.

Chapter 4
Gifts

Gifts

After a short, private deliberation, the judges decided unanimously. Akwa won the competition. She received a precious symbol as a prize: a long, thin, pale blue shell pendant, shaped like a horn, which was hung on a necklace around her neck. It enhanced her delicate beauty. One of the female village elders presented it to her in a ritual ceremony, and as the audience cheered and applauded her, the elder pulled her close and told Akwa of its sacred and magical properties that would protect her when she needed it most.

Of course, Akwa also had the honour of being the one chosen to go on the quest to the other side of the island to seek the advice of Zandra, the Wise Woman. Zandra could advise the village what to do now that the three signs had been fulfilled, as the villagers' interpretations were too different, and no one could decide which path of action to take.

Akwa was terrified by the prospect of the journey and didn't want to go alone. The track would be dangerous, going across tall mountains where she would lose sight and sound of the sea. She was worried that she might get lost and never find her way home again. She shared her fears with her mother, and Moana sat down with her and gave Akwa another seashell necklace. The shell itself was round and pearly white, with a silver circular spiral etched around it, and a small hole in the middle.

"This shell has been a family heirloom for generations. It is our lucky charm, and it will bring you creative inspiration when you most need it," said her mother.

Akwa didn't understand, but she accepted the precious gift and prepared for her journey. As she packed, her friends and family gave her food, shoes, clothing, a sleeping mat and, of course, advice.

"Don't you think you will need a map? So you know where to go?" said practical Kiwi.

"Look out for the monkeys who might grab your necklace!" teased Uluru playfully.

"Watch out for the Red Dragon Trolls!" warned Kriti.

"Oh, they don't exist. They're just stories to scare children," Akwa replied.

The Big Picture

Moana took Akwa to see the village elders, as they had some knowledge about the island which was passed down from their ancestors. As they entered into the dimly lit cave of the elders, which Akwa had never been inside before, she noticed that the walls were covered with runes and other strange symbols. Some of them she could understand, as Moana had shown individual runes to her, but there were so many, and they were drawn higgledy-piggledy on top of each other, some of them framed into whole pictures.

"What do they all mean, Moana?" she whispered.

"No one knows anymore. Unfortunately we lost the key to deciphering the meanings of the symbols," said Moana.

"Oh! Where did you lose the key?" asked Akwa innocently.

Her mother didn't reply as an old man appeared. He ushered them into an inner room which had a circle of stools with two empty ones nearest them. He indicated silently that they were to sit.

Akwa looked at the six elders in the circle. They were the oldest and wisest people in the village, which included Moana. *And it used to include Tahi, too,* thought Akwa sadly.

The elders welcomed the two women, and there was a short ceremony to acknowledge Akwa as the winner of the dance competition and chosen to represent the village.

At the conclusion of the ritual, one of the elder women gave Akwa a map of Bula Island with landmarks, reference points, walking paths and her trail marked on it so she could find her way across the mountains to Zandra's house somewhere on the other side of the island. Akwa noticed that the island was shaped like a crescent moon.

"Thank you! I appreciate having this map. It gives me the big picture of the island. Akwa was very grateful. "But why can't I go by sea?" she asked, thinking it must be quicker and less treacherous than crossing the mountains.

"Well, first of all, the boats are all broken," said one of the male elders.

"Secondly, the storms would blow you away, as the winds are all blowing offshore," said another elder. "You could get blown out to sea, so you must go by land."

"But why do I have to go over the big, tall mountains in the middle of the island?" queried Akwa.

"That is the only way to the other side of the island where the wise woman lives. Pela the Mountain Goddess will help you and protect you."

Chapter 5

Journey

The Journey Begins

Early the next morning, Akwa set out on her quest. She was fondly farewelled by the villagers. Her friends Kiwi, Ulura and Leilani followed her along the path until they got to the Gateway. This was an ancient stone arch which shadowed the path. Children were strictly forbidden by their parents to go anywhere past this foreboding marker, where the path which led to the other side of the island began.

Unimaginable dangers lurked beyond, and the path was narrow and windy, quickly disappearing out of sight amongst the dark jungle trees. Akwa slowly moved through the Gateway expecting at any moment for it to fall down on her, or something jump out at her from the other side.

With fear and trepidation, she started along the narrow path. Then she turned and waved to her friends who waved back sadly as they moved out of her sight. The path gently grew steeper and wider as she climbed along it, up into the foothills. Initially she enjoyed the gentle, winding trail, which was smooth despite not many people using it. *Perhaps it's used by animals*, Akwa thought anxiously. Exotic tropical trees lined the edges of the path, and occasionally she saw bright flowers or the flash of a bird's wings.

***

On her first night alone, Akwa could not sleep, tossing and turning, terrified by all the sounds of the bush: crazy chirping of crickets' wings and "who-cooks-for-you" hooting of owls. She jumped in fright when she heard knocking sounds from strange night birds, and the *ribbit ribbit* of frogs calling to their mates. Eventually, as the night reached its darkest, the familiar sound of sea waves gently washing across the shore lulled her to a restful sleep.

Over the next two days she walked up hills and down into deep, dark valleys, leading her through the verdant rain forest. At dusk she always found a clearing at the edge of the path. *It's as if they were designed and planned to be there beside the path,* she mused.

***

One morning, shortly after setting off from her camp, Akwa's path meandered toward a beautiful waterfall and stream, with large boulders she could use to cross. A childish joy filled her as her crossing became a game. Leaping from boulder to boulder, she laughed at the fun of flitting from rock to rock. As she neared the spray of the waterfall, one of the boulders she landed on was slippery, and she lost her footing, sending Akwa careening into the water.

She sank like a stone, her travelling gear weighing her down. As she drifted down, she glimpsed something sparkling at the bottom of a deep, blue hole. She paused a moment to look longer, trying to make out what the object was, before running out of breath and kicking toward the surface.

Magic Treasure

Akwa emerged into the air, lungs burning as she spluttered, blinking water out of her eyes. She dragged herself to shore, dumped her belongings in a sodden pile beside her, before lying on her back to catch her breath. *Hopefully,* she mused, *they'll be dry before I need them to sleep tonight.*

She glanced back at the water, then rolled her eyes. *Oh, I really should forget about this. I don't have time to stop and hunt for lost treasure.* But it was only a short stop, what harm could it do? She groaned, and knew it was foolish.

The waterfall crashed behind her as she climbed to her feet and undressed, leaving her clothes to dry in the midday sun. She shook some warmth into her limbs, took a deep breath, then threw herself back in. Without the shock of the cold, Akwa dove down in strong strokes, the gleam and shine of something below pulling her closer. It was nestled inside a hole, and as she neared, she realised it was just wide enough for her to squeeze through.

The rock scraped her shoulders as she pushed through, the pressure of being so deep making her ears hurt, but she ignored it as she reached for the treasure. Her fingers curled around a gold ring, and she raised it up to her eye as she hung suspended in the water. It was cold, perfectly preserved.

Something shifted in the water around her, and as her focus moved from the ring to her surroundings, two red eyes peered at her from the gloom. Akwa dropped the ring as a red snout snarled toward her, teeth bared. *It can't be. They're just stories Moana told around the fire.* She turned, tried to kick off the riverbed and back to the surface, but a strong, taloned claw gripped her ankle and yanked her back. Bubbles burst from her lips, and against her better instinct, Akwa screamed as she was dragged roughly back through the hole. Just before the water rushed into her lungs, dissolving her consciousness to black, a single thought chased her into the beast's lair. *Moana was right. Red Dragon Trolls are real.*

Chapter 6

Red Dragon Troll

Captured by the **Red Dragon Troll**

Akwa came to in a daze. As her vision cleared, she found that she was tied up, held gently by strong, silken strands like a spider's web. Looking around, she saw that she was lying in a soft, spongy, oval cocoon at the bottom of a cave, an air bubble haloed around her head so that she could breathe, her arms and fingers, toes and feet exposed to the cool, clear water. She lay there, fearfully awaiting her fate, shivering and shaking, her eyes as big as saucers and unable to move, scream or even talk.

The Red Dragon Troll enjoyed arranging and rearranging her legs and arms. It stroked and tickled her fingers and toes while it crooned a song about fresh, tender morsels; crunchy, tiny, twinkling toes and the delicacy of dainty digits.

Akwa trembled with fear at the thought of the loss of her fingers and their healing touch. She imagined her toeless, bleeding feet, and, worst of all, the failure of her quest. She felt deeply disappointed at letting down her family, friends and community, and they would never know what had happened to her.

However, when she looked closely at the Red Dragon Troll, she saw that its appendages were ragged. It seemed that what could have been legs, arms, hands or feet were missing. She realised that because it had lost its own legs, arms, toes and fingers, that it was feeling the trauma of their loss and longing for its missing parts. When she identified with the pain of separation, a wave of emotion flowed through her, and she felt the shift of her energy, changing to compassion then to unconditional love and healing.

The Red Dragon Troll looked into her eyes and saw her compassion, and tears came into its red eyes as it began to babble its story.

It had once lived in the sea with the goddess, but it loved to tease the fishermen by grabbing onto the boats with its fingers and toes and shaking them.

The fishermen were very afraid and would wail in fear. One day, a brave fisherman leaned over and chopped off the troll's fingers and toes. In pain, the troll sank to the bottom of the ocean and hid in the depths of the coral reef, nursing its hurt feet and hands while its anger grew. It would burst up and hit the fishermen's boats hard with its head and knock the men into the water, snapping at their fingers and toes. It wanted them to know how it felt.

With shame in its voice, the troll told how the sea goddess was very cross with the Red Dragon Troll for harming the dedicated fishermen. Although she said she had valued the troll, she knew it couldn't stay in the ocean while it was so angry, so she had sent it away, ordered to follow a little stream that emptied into the sea. It had slowly slithered up the stream into the mountains until it found the waterfall and little water hole where it had lived ever since, remaining there and eating the toes and fingers of anyone it could catch.

Listening to this sad, difficult story, Akwa noticed tears flowing from her eyes and rolling down her cheeks. They fell on the white shell necklace, which was flashing in the light of the Red Dragon Troll's eyes. Suddenly the cave was lit with a wonderful glow.

Akwa and the troll were bathed in the light. With wonder and joy, they watched the toes and fingers of the troll growing again, healing both his body and his heart. The release of his anger had drained the red colour from his body, and it changed, back to its original beautiful jade green.

"You're a Jade Sea Dragon," marvelled Akwa as she recognised his primal shape. "I have seen drawings of you in our caves!"

As the light faded, the happy and proud Jade Sea Dragon unravelled the silken strand constraints and released her.

"*You are the Chosen One,*" a soft voice spoke in Akwa's head. "*You wear the sacred magic necklace. You have a special purpose, and you are loved by Sedna the Sea Goddess.*"

Akwa sighed with relief, suddenly able to find her voice. "It is true, I am on my way to see the wise woman on the other side of the mountains." Then she laughed bitterly. "But love? No. The sea goddess took away my father, and I cannot forgive her. She doesn't love me."

"*You have a bigger destiny than you or your friends and family could ever imagine,*" the Jade Sea Dragon murmured. "*You have healed me, and I am very grateful. I do not wish to feast on your fingers or toes, or anyone's fingers or toes, or harm you in any way.*"

"I must not delay you anymore. You can swim out through my Blue Grotto and pick up your belongings to resume your quest," the Jade Sea Dragon said in her head.

"Thank you," breathed Akwa with a sigh of relief.

"I must compensate you for delaying you, Chosen One," the Jade Sea Dragon said to Akwa. *"Here are my gifts that you will need when the time is right."*

Red Coral Jewel

The Jade Sea Dragon pointed to a small shelf on the wall of the cave, indicating that she take the three things nestled there: a small piece of curiously shaped red coral which was round at one end and smaller and shaped at the other end; a soft, silvery gossamer ball; and a red cloth bag to put them both in. Akwa hung the bag on her belt, then together they swam out through the Blue Grotto and up into the sunlight.

At the surface, the Jade Sea Dragon stopped and listened. "*Akwa, I can hear the ocean,*" a softer, sweeter voice sang in her head.

It turned in a trice and quickly began to swim down the stream towards the ocean. The goddess was calling her Jade Sea Dragon home.

Akwa dressed into dry clothes, sorted out her soaked belongings and left a couple of brightly coloured shells by the steppingstones. Then she discarded some of the precious but heavy things she didn't need for the rest of her journey. She picked up remainder and set off along the path, which snaked across the foothills and into the mountains as she followed the map's directions.

***

Up and up she climbed, and the rainforest gave way to small, scrubby trees, which thinned out and became increasingly sparse, replaced with big boulders and maroon-coloured volcanic rocks. Eventually, Akwa reached the high cloud-covered mountains where there were no trees. Just bare, black rocks. The path was marked by smaller stones along the edge, and sometimes it was just a narrow groove that she followed. In exposed places it was very windy, and she had to step carefully on the damp rocks to avoid slipping again. She could no longer hear the sound of the sea as she was so far away, just the wind in her ears and the scuff of her feet on the trail.

Although she had clues when she looked at the map she was given, she wasn't prepared for the panoramic view. It was unlike anything she'd ever imagined. To her left, the village looked so tiny and far away. She could see some of the destruction caused by the tsunami: flattened and uprooted trees, debris everywhere amid the shattered remnants of her home and wreckage of the fishing boats. To her right, she could see part of the other side of the island that she had never seen before. There were more mountains, plunging steeply into the sea on both sides. Further over, the hills sloped down into the tropical rainforest again, with a couple of empty little beaches on the lagoon side.

When she looked behind her, to the south, she could see the vastness of the crystal-clear blue ocean, all the way to where the azure sky merged with the hazy horizon. She sat down on a rock and watched until the sea birds came back to the island in the twilight, wheeling and calling to each other, coming home in the rich red clouds of the sunset.

Coming home! She missed her village, her home and the cosiness that her parents had created for her with their love. It was all washed away with the other parts of the village. She even missed her temporary home that she and Moana had set up together in their allocated cave. And still she yearned for Tahi's enveloping love.

Again, she did not sleep well that night. She tossed and turned. Her necklaces twisted, and her ear touched the round shell. Suddenly she could hear sound of the waves on the beach, softly lapping on the seashore. She tuned in to it and held the shell to her ear, listening. Then she heard the storm surf on the rocks, the waves breaking and crashing on the coral reef. Lulled by these familiar sounds, she dreamed that she saw her father happily riding on the waves with two dolphins. The message he gave her echoed in her head.

"Do not reject me for I am your provider. I give you food, rain, inspiration, joy and pleasure. I give you my gifts of new life and unconditional love. I send you love from the sea goddess."

For the first time in many months, Akwa was at peace with Sedna. Although she was far away from her foam and spray, she knew that the sea goddess would always be with her. Wrapped in love and a feeling of forgiveness, she felt calmed by her inner peace.

ic

Chapter 7
Pela

Meeting Pela

All the following day, Akwa walked on the bare, rocky path across the mountains, up into the clouds and mist. It was so high and foggy that she couldn't even see the sea anymore. Her path, edged by sharp stones, led through deep rocky passes which towered over her as she walked through the dark valleys.

The next night, she slept in a small cave that she found beside the path. She dreamed that Pela the Mountain Goddess came to her. Akwa knew that Pela was a red volcanic goddess who creates new islands from the lava that flows from her fingertips, though Akwa did not remember exactly what she had looked like in her dream when she woke up.

In the dream, Pela told Akwa to go to the back of the cave and walk through the arched portal that she found there, where she would be able to enter the Mountain Temple to receive an initiation and healing.

The next morning, after eating the last of her food, Akwa explored the cave that she had slept in. She lit a torch and walked towards the deep recesses of the cave. She did indeed find an archway, and slowly walked through it along a level path that had been carved out of the rock.

Eventually she came out into a huge, open cavern, where three archways enclosed three triangular alcoves. Each alcove was painted – one was white for Sedna, one was red for Pela and one was black for Gaia. At the bottom of each alcove offering bowls were carved into the stone. She put her torch in a niche in the wall and its light illuminated the whole cavern.

Akwa did a gratitude ritual without even realising it. She invoked Sedna, Gaia and

Pela, thanking them for her safety, then she sent love to her family and friends, and asked for the goddesses' blessings for the remainder of her journey. She burned some incense she found there and sat down before closing her eyes and slipping into a meditative trance, lulled by the powerful energy of the Mountain Temple.

Pela's Healing

Akwa had a vision that Pela appeared in front of her. The goddess was huge, and she had glowing red hair, with sparks coming out of her eyes and the tips of her fingers. She wore a long black and red dress which covered her toes. Akwa felt apprehensive, confronted by Pela's mighty powerful energy. However, she sat still with anticipation. Pela came towards Akwa and touched the centre of her forehead with her finger. It glowed and burned in the shape of a star, but it did not hurt Akwa as it was energetic.

"This healing has activated your third eye so that you can become a more powerful transformational healer," breathed Pela. *"When you invoke the goddess, you need to fill yourself with healing energy first, then when it overflows you can send it into the person's heart and body with unconditional love and healing for them.*

You will need these extra healing powers very soon for a special person you will meet..." she said mysteriously. *"When you are healing, you need to tune in to the essence and spirit of the element of the person you are healing. These elements are earth, fire, water, wood or metal. This will enhance the healing process."*

"Namaste, Pela." Akwa thanked her with reverence, and she felt awed, but also honoured and enlightened, by the presence of the goddess. When she opened her eyes, the vision of Pela was gone. However, her forehead still tingled from the warm energy of her gentle but powerful touch. *Like a steel hand in a velvet glove,* thought Akwa.

Chapter 8

Shakir

Shakir the Monkey Shaman

In the afternoon, Akwa walked along the path and down the other side of the mountains, the path meandered down to the moist green rainforest. Now the edges of the path were marked by smooth stones of many colours. As she got closer to the sea, the edges became beautiful shells, different from any Akwa had seen before. Finally, she came to a clearing where there were three raised platforms with thatched roofs.

She saw that they were set in a triangular shape with a pole in the middle. There were beautiful bright flowers in neat gardens on the edges of the three paths that ran between the platforms and met at the pole. It looked and felt homely, and Akwa felt safe and at ease there.

Checking her map, she found that she needed to go straight through this area. She stepped into the clearing. Suddenly, a horde of noisy monkeys ran towards her and started pulling off all her belongings, and even her clothes. She struggled but was soon totally naked. The cheeky monkeys ran away and climbed up on one of the higher platforms. All Akwa wore now were her two necklaces and waist belt with the red bag that the Jade Sea Dragon had given her.

One of the monkeys had tried to grab her precious belt away, but she managed to regain it by snatching it back and hooking the strap tightly around her wrist, not wanting to relinquish the priceless treasures it contained. Then she held it protectively over her hips, and crossed her arms, the universal sign of fear.

As she looked around at the platforms, confused and anxious, torn between wanting to run away to escape the monkeys' grasping hands and the need to get her belongings back, a tall man appeared beside the centre pole. He had a long white beard and wore a tall hat with strange symbols on it. His long cloak shimmered in the sunlight. He spoke several words, but she did not understand the language. Then he tried sign language, but still Akwa did not understand.

Then he pointed to her belt, to which she had tied the red cloth bag. He indicated that she should open it and take something out. *The gossamer? No. The red coral? Of course!* Then the stranger indicated that she put it in her left ear. It was the perfect size and shape. When she did, he spoke again. This time she could understand exactly what he was saying.

"Greetings, Chosen One! I welcome you to Aloha. I am Shakir, the monkey shaman. I am one of your guides on your quest. My spirit guides told me you were on your way. I have seen many signs, and I have been eagerly waiting for your visit. Come and wash your weary body. My monkeys will keep you safe and look after your needs. Then you can drink and eat your fill with me."

Akwa climbed up onto the platform he indicated. Carefully, she put down her bag and red coral earpiece beside a huge clam shell. It was full of warm fresh water, so she gratefully bathed the travel dust from her body and washed her hair. Afterwards she dressed in a clean sarong which was provided for her and put the translation earpiece into her ear again.

On the second, lower platform, Shakir and Akwa ate together. It was a delicious feast of fresh food: baked fish, fresh tropical fruit and vegetables and coconut water. After satiating her hunger and thirst, she felt weary. Shakir indicated that she could rest on the third platform.

When she finally crawled up to the third platform, all her belongings were there, cleaned and neatly folded for her. And there was a beautiful, soft bed, which she reclined upon and quickly fell asleep.

That night, Akwa dreamed that a beautiful woman came to her and showed her a special dance. It was a dance of mermaids or sirens who danced on top of the waves of the sea and skimmed from wave to wave. In the background, silvery flute-like music played. She could hear it but could not see the source of the beautiful sounds. Akwa woke up from the dream with the haunting music still playing in her head.

Chapter 9

Zandra

The Lagoon and the Wise Woman's House

Shakir the monkey shaman greeted her the next morning, and they ate delicious banana pancakes together. The monkeys sat around them, eating bananas and chatting quietly.

Akwa was curious to know how her clothes were washed and dried. Shakir told her that the monkeys were responsible. "Thank you, kind monkeys," said Akwa with gratitude. The monkeys looked happy and put their palms together in a namaste sign to her.

Shakir invited Akwa to join him after she had visited the Wise Woman. "Last night my spirit guides told me that you need to meet my apprentice. At present, he is receiving healing for his strong headaches, but he will be back in a few days. You will know when to come back and see him." Akwa thanked Shakir and the monkeys for their hospitality and agreed to return. The monkeys gave her some bananas for her journey.

*****

Akwa walked along the sandy path which led north from Shakir's platforms between rows of palm trees and coconut trees. A few hours later, as the trees changed to grasses and then to sandy beach, she could hear the gentle lapping of the water on the shallow shelly beach of the lagoon. She ran towards the water, shedding her bags and clothes, and jumped into the crystal-clear water, splashing around and diving under. Doing dolphin dives, she skimmed along the sandy bottom, and floated on the gentle waves, to finally lie in the shallows of the foamy edge in the sea.

"Oh, I missed your calmness, your sound, your taste, your touch," she whispered to the sea.

And the sea goddess might have sighed back, "*I missed you too, beloved.*"

Suddenly, two dolphins jumped out of the lagoon. A mother and baby dolphin leaped clear. They made a rainbow ark of water above the surface of the lagoon, creating the illusion of a circular spiral in the shimmering air. Akwa clapped her hands in delight.

Cool and happy, she gathered her belongings and walked along the shore, collecting shells that caught her eye and storing them in her red bag. There were many long thin ones similar to the blue shell on her necklace.

Finally, Akwa arrived at a beautiful house made of local bamboo. It was decorated with shells, feathers and colourful flowers. Outside sat a woman with long beautiful hair. Silver strands wove among her iron-grey hair, with a red streak in the front, and feathers and tiny shells decorating the ends. She wore a loose brightly coloured dress of rainbow hues like Akwa had never seen before.

Zandra the Wise Woman

The woman looked up and said, "Welcome, Akwa. I've been expecting you. Here is a cool coconut drink to refresh you."

Akwa put her palms together and said, "Aloha. Thank you. You must be Zandra?" As she sipped the fresh sweet coconut juice, she found herself relaxing, feeling happy that she had finally arrived at her destination.

"Yes, I am Zandra. How can I help you? What healing do you desire?"

Akwa gave a contented sigh. She felt very safe and comfortable in Zandra's presence.

She first told Zandra about the dolphins jumping in the lagoon, as she hadn't seen them there for many years. Zandra said that the huge wave – the tsunami – had washed all the dangerous sea creatures out of the lagoon, and the dolphins were a sign that the lagoon was safe to travel across to the village.

Akwa told her about her village by the sea, her father's disappearance, about the storms and the winds, the huge wave, and the destruction of the houses and fishing boats. She said that her mother, Moana, had told her that that these were the signs from the runes in the Caves of the Ancients. Akwa said that she was chosen to visit Zandra, seeking her advice for the future of the village.

Zandra listened without interrupting until Akwa came to the end of her tale.

"Yes, Moana is correct. These are the Three Ultimate Signs foretold by your ancestors. The man lost to the sea, the destructive tsunami and the fruiting tree."

"But what do these signs mean?" asked Akwa.

Akwa's Quest Explained

Zandra told her that, many years ago, Moana had made a special prayer for a child at the sea temple at the full moon. It was a blood moon, when the moon took on a reddish colour. The next day, Tahi found a baby on the beach washed up in a strange yellow boat. Moana and Tahi looked after her as if she was their own child. The name on the yellow boat was "Artiye", but it was too hard to pronounce so they called her Akwa.

"Yes, I know that story. Moana and Tahi told me it when I was younger. I know that I am a special being, but they didn't tell me *why* I'm special. I know that I'm different to other children my age. I often have strange dreams about flying among the stars," said Akwa.

"You *are* a child of the stars, Akwa," said Zandra, "The night before your father found you, everyone saw a comet fly across the sky, and I remember it clearly. You are the chosen one for many reasons, and your destiny is much bigger than this island. You must continue on your journey and sail with the sea traders to other lands. Your quest on this world is to do a special study of the inhabitants and report back to your High Priestess."

Akwa's eyes grew wider and wider with this information. She was trying to understand what Zandra was saying – it sounded like a tale from the ancient runes in the caves that Moana had told her. But Moana had never mentioned anything like this!

Zandra continued. "These signs mean that the time is right for you to leave the island and begin your quest. There are instructions for you in your yellow pod boat, which came from your starship."

Akwa was dazed, amazed and astonished. Her head was still spinning with this strange, new information. Yet, deep inside, she felt it was true. Small threads of memory awakened in her being, remembering her dreams of impossibly beautiful people and inexplicable experiences. She had always thought they were just dreams and had dismissed them.

Zandra and Akwa sat in meditation together on the shore by the quiet lagoon. Akwa needed to absorb and integrate this amazing information that Zandra had just given her.

They talked at length about Akwa's bigger quest, and Zandra answered as many questions as she could. Then they ate a simple seafood and mango salad and went to sleep under the stars, which looked the same, but now felt very different to Akwa.

The Meaning of the Gifts

The next day, after a lovely banana pancake and fresh fruit for breakfast, Akwa told

Zandra about her journey across the island – the Jade Sea Dragon troll and the red coral jewel, the gossamer, her vision in Pela's cave and her dream about the music of the sea.

Zandra listened, then she said, "Show me the gifts you were given by the Jade Sea Dragon." Akwa took the red jewel stone and gossamer from the red bag on her belt.

"First show me the gossamer, Akwa," said Zandra. "Gossamer from spider webs can sanitise and heal open wounds. This is a powerful healing gift from the Jade Sea Dragon.

"The red jewel stone is a translation crystal to help you understand different languages…"

"Like Shakir's," Akwa interrupted excitedly.

"Yes. And it can also to help you interpret the words of the heart, which are often unspoken because of people's emotions and feelings. Now you can help people express these emotions safely for their healing. Notice that your necklace and the red jewel stone have the same pattern on them - the eighth path spiral."

"Ooh, yes!" Akwa exclaimed. 'What does it mean?"

"It means that they originally came from the same place – the ancient people who lived on this island and built the caves," said Zandra.

"And where did they come from?"

"From the stars."

"Aah, so my ancestors have been here before?" Akwa asked, stunned.

The Sea Players

Zandra confirmed with a gentle nod. "The woman in your dream is Sedna the Sea Goddess. She misses you and wants you to play for her, because you are a Sea Player, and you make her favourite music for her to dance to."

Akwa frowned. "But how do I make the music that I heard in my dream? I have no instrument to play."

"Yes, you do." Zandra looked at Akwa kindly. "The solution is in front of you. It's hanging on your two necklaces. Take them off and show me."

Surprised, Akwa took off her necklaces for the first time since they were given to her. Zandra showed her how the long thin shell was the same size as the hole in the centre of the round white one. The blue shell fit into the hole in the centre, and it made sounds, music. When she put it to her lips, an elusive, flute-like tune played, just like in her dream. Akwa danced happily to the music, and the waves danced, the sun sparkled on the lagoon as again two dolphins leaped out of the water.

"You need to play to the sea every day," said Zandra. "You can collect these shells from the north-eastern beach, which is beyond that tree. Take them home and teach your friends how to play this flute for Sedna."

"The sea goddess will be happy," said Akwa and Zandra simultaneously, and they smiled at each other.

Zandra's Wisdom

Akwa stayed with Zandra for one moon cycle. She learnt more about the timing and healing powers of the five elements – metal, earth, water, fire and air. She discovered that each element had a colour and was represented by an elemental goddess.

First there was the Blue Wise Woman who ruled over deep water and winter – as represented by Sedna the Sea Goddess. The silver, metallic Moon Goddess's name was Silver Alchemiste, because, like moonlight, she stripped away any unworthiness, transformed it and left only the pure valuable silver.

Zandra personified the empathic healing Earth Mother, and Pela the Earth Goddess, whose golden-brown earthiness connects people and helps them feel grounded in autumn. The playful shaman's monkeys represented the fairies who lived in the green trees of the forests and represented the Amazon nature, devas and spring.

Lastly, fire was the element for the Red Sun Goddess, who uplifts and warms with her joy and love in summer.

Zandra taught her about the moon phases and when the best time is for planting crops. They were walking among a small grove of fruit trees that Zandra had grown as she shared her wisdom. "At the New Moon, make your four wishes and intentions that you want to happen in two weeks at the Full Moon. Plant root crops four days before the New Moon. Plant above ground crops, like green leafy herbs and vegetables, two days after the New Moon.

"The time of the Full Moon is for taking action and manifesting, so it's a good time to sow edible sprouts for about three days after the full moon, and two days to sow root crops, such as sweet potatoes. The Last Quarter is the best time for harvesting, maintenance, weeding, pruning, cultivating and fertilising."

Akwa enjoyed learning these synchronicities and absorbed the information like a sponge. She was excited to take this information back to the villagers to improve their food cultivation and harvests.

Spiritual Guidance and Cleansing

Zandra also taught her how to keep her spiritual essence cleansed and high. "It's easy – just three steps," she said. "First you think of your highest desire or favourite thing. For example: love, joy, happiness, or maybe even mango. What is it?"

Without hesitation, Akwa replied, "Love."

Zandra continued. "So, step one is to repeat this mantra to yourself – out loud or quietly, you decide which. *In the name of love, I cleanse my body and my soul.*"

Akwa echoed the mantra. "In the name of love, I cleanse my body and my soul."

"The second step is to rub your hands together three or four times to energise your aura. Then put your two middle fingers together in the centre of your forehead, about where you think your third eye is, and gently trace your fingers around the edge of your face to your chin in a circle. Bring your palms together in a namaste. Then put your fingers back onto the middle of your forehead again, and this time trace your fingers together over the back of your head, and down to the centre of the back of your neck. Separate them around your neck and bring them to the front into namaste.

"The final step is that to pull your hands apart and shake them. This will help to energise them. Do these steps a few times, until it's a smooth motion.

"While you're doing these actions, say to yourself, *In the name of love, I cleanse my body and I cleanse my soul.* As you say *my body*, put your hands around your face, then as you say *my soul* move your hands behind your head and your neck."

Zandra told her to repeat this, two or three times every day, or until she felt relaxed, energised and happy.

Over the next few days Akwa used the spiritual cleansing and energizing practice often: when she was feeling upset - sad or angry - or when she felt lonely and missed her friends and family. It always made her feel better, more connected and more grounded. And she couldn't wait to teach her friends and family this simple little spiritual cleansing technique!

Zandra also showed Akwa how to communicate with her spirit guides and ask them questions that would otherwise not be able to be answered.

"It takes practice to get clear spiritual guidance," she told Akwa. "Mostly it's about asking the correct questions."

Love and Relationships

Zandra had an interesting book about loving and relationships, and Akwa was very interested in it. When she read it, she felt an excitement and a familiarity about the information that she didn't understand.

There were many lessons about masculine and feminine energy, control and weaving together initiation rituals, intimacy, massage and healing. She read about unconditional love; sacred feminine; womb magic; water magic; shell songs and many other fascinating topics.

Akwa was enthusiastically anticipating using her newfound knowledge, and it inspired her to want to learn and experience more about energy and relationships.

Sedna the Sea Goddess

Zandra told Akwa many more stories about Sedna the Sea Goddess. One of the stories was gruesome because it mentioned that Sedna had chopped off people's fingers and toes! However, they became seals, dolphins and whales, so there was a good outcome. *Maybe it was a metaphor,* mused Akwa.

And of course, Akwa and Zandra played music and sang to Sedna the Sea Goddess every day at Zandra's personal ocean temple.

***

One night, Akwa dreamed that her father was calling her from the dark depths of the sea, but she could not find him because there was a wall of shells held together by woven seaweed blocking her way.

First thing the next morning, she told Zandra about her prophetic dream.

"Is that a sign that you need to take some action?" asked Zandra.

Akwa nodded. "I promised to go back and visit Shakir and the monkeys. I will go and see them today," Akwa told Zandra excitedly.

"Don't forget to take your necklaces and healing bag," said Zandra. Akwa's red bag that the Jade Sea Dragon had given her was now full of healing herbs that Zandra had taught Akwa how to use.

Chapter: 10
Akir

The Apprentice

Akwa happily skipped up the shell-edged path to Shakir's settlement. The shaman's monkeys welcomed her back with tasty bananas, and Shakir waited for her at the entrance of the clearing accompanied by another man.

"I would like you to meet my apprentice, Akir." He introduced a tall, slim man who *felt* vaguely familiar, although Akwa did not recognise him. He was dressed like Shakir in traditional, long, shapeless shamanic robes.

Akir had very long, untidy hair, a straggly, knotted beard and an unusual hat with long sides on his head. He had a strange, rasping way of speaking the same language as Shakir. Akwa needed to use the red coral translator in her ear so she could understand his words more clearly.

They sat together on the lower platform, which was like a square gazebo. It had a thatched roof of coconut fronds, and it was raised above the sand. The base was covered with earthy-coloured woven mats and plump, soft cushions. It was set up for entertaining – on a low table rested a tray with three glasses of fresh juice and some sweet nuts and dried bananas for them to nibble on.

Akir told her that he didn't know how he got there. He couldn't remember anything before the monkeys found him on the beach and took him to Shakir. He had no language then, but Shakir had taught him his shamanic language and given him the name Akir. Then Shakir began to train him as an apprentice, because, even without words, he learnt quickly and was very intelligent.

Akir said that he often got very hot, even if the weather was cold, and he was easily confused. He suffered from migraines which were worse when the weather was stormy. He also reported that his headaches often made it hard for him to concentrate and learn his shamanic lessons.

Shakir had advised him to go to the High Mountain Temple for healing with Pela the Mountain Goddess, as he believed that Pela could cleanse and revive his recent past, reconnecting him to his memory. Additionally, Shakir had hoped she would help Akir with his amnesia, migraines and other symptoms. However, after seven days of practicing the rituals that Shakir had recommended, very little had changed, other than that Akir felt more at peace in himself.

Akwa said, "Pela communicated with me at the High Mountain Temple and strengthened my healing abilities on my journey across the island. I am also connected to Sedna the Sea

Goddess as a water healer. I would like to help you with your healing. Is that OK with you?"

"Yes," Akir confirmed. "What would that involve? Would it hurt me? I don't want any more pain. I would appreciate some gentle healing." He was a bit apprehensive and very nervous.

"My healing is very gentle and energetic, with a light touch," Akwa reassured him. "Today I would merely like to stroke your hair and hold your head, which might help with your migraines and assist you in remembering your memories. Do you consent to that?"

"Yes, of course! I hope it will relieve some of my pain." He took off his hat and lay down on the mat, and Akwa cradled the back of his head with her hands. Akwa gently put her index fingers on his occiput at the base of his skull. She felt her fingertips pulse as an electrical wave of energy flowed through her fingertips into his head. They were silent for a while to enable the healing process. Akwa held his head and gently stroked his hair. She felt him relax with her healing touch, and she focused on channelling the healing energy down her body, down her arms and into her hands. When she intuitively knew he had received enough healing for his first session, she gently placed his head on a pillow and moved to gently hold his ankles to ground him. As she watched, she saw that he was so relaxed he might have been asleep.

After the healing, Akwa told him about her quest and her visit to Zandra. She told Akir that she missed her mother, Moana. No sooner had he heard the word *Moana*, he suddenly said, "*Aloha amor mau loa*" which means *I love you forever.*

Akwa said, "What an unusual thing to say! My father used to say that to my mother."

Then, as she was an empath, and being in tune with his energy, Akwa looked closely into his eyes – the pathway to his heart – and recognised Akir as her father, Tahi.

Akwa felt a range of emotions flow through her – relief that she had found her dad, sadness that he was not aware of her, happiness that he was actually alive, and joy for her mother, family and the rest of the community. She contained her excitement when she realised that he did not notice her awareness.

Unfortunately, Akir didn't recognise her because he had amnesia from hitting his head when he fell off his boat, and his soul had separated into two parts. Akwa intuitively knew that it was an aspect of her quest to help heal him so that he would be whole again and fully remember his language and family. This was just the beginning of his healing.

***

Shakir confirmed that the gossamer would also help to heal a wound on Akir's head. She put some of her precious gossamer on his head to protect it, seal it and heal it, and she changed it often.

Every day until the next full moon, Akwa went to visit Akir. Gradually, it was her words, her love and her care that helped him heal and remember himself.

Akir's Dream

One day, Akir told Akwa about a dream he had the previous night. He dreamt that he was a fisherman who had caught a big fish, except the fish was so big that it pulled him into the water. He remembered hitting his head and then sinking to the bottom of the ocean. A beautiful woman with sea blue-green hair had given him a special shell to put in his ear so that he could understand her.

Akwa looked in his ears and found a piece of seaweed in one of them. She carefully pulled on it, then stopped. "Does that hurt, Akir?"

"It's uncomfortable but it just tickles a bit," he replied.

"I am going to pull it out. I'll take it slowly and easily."

So Akwa gently pulled a bit more, rested, and pulled gently again. Finally, it unwound and at the end was a tiny shell. When she pulled it out, Akir's memory was restored. He sat quietly for a moment, then he looked around as if seeing Akwa, the rainforest and the gazebo for the first time. Then he stood up and looked at her and said, "Akwa! Oh, my lovely daughter, Akwa! I remember you. My memories have come back."

Emotionally, Akwa responded, "I have missed you so much!"

They hugged each other for a long time.

Akwa was ecstatically happy. *He finally remembers me!*

And he remembered Moana too, and asked how she was. He also realised that his name was Tahi, and that he was a fisherman from the village on the other side of the island. As they hugged each other they both felt the joy, tears and laughter of being reunited. They danced and sang and celebrated.

***

When they told Shakir, he wept with tears of gratitude that Akir had remembered his past and was reunited with his loving daughter. He suggested that Akir be known in future as Tahi-Akir, and Tahi was pleased with this suggestion. He also said that he had retained all the shamanic teachings and practices that Shakir had taught him. Tahi-Akir passionately wanted to be a shaman and teach the young men from his village the shaman's knowledge.

Then, with emotional tears of joy, they went and told Zandra. "We must celebrate this reunion!" she said. And the four had a celebration with lots of delicious food and dancing and fun together.

Building a Canoe

Once Akir realised he was Tahi, more of his memories began to come back. Combined with his awakened shaman intuition and psychic abilities, he felt whole and happy again. He wanted to create and build something, a new project.

"We can build a boat to go home!" he said excitedly to Akwa.

They set off into the jungle to find a suitable hollow tree for the hull of the canoe. The monkeys came too. They could communicate with Tahi-Akir and he understood them, so he sent them out to find a suitable fallen tree.

"They've found three!" he exclaimed to Akwa when the monkeys returned.

However, the first one was too big and couldn't be moved by two people, so they left it where it lay. The second one was too short and too thick to be used for a boat, but it made a nice chimney for Zandra's cooking fire.

The third one was perfect. Tahi-Akir stripped the bark off the outside, then he burned small fires in the wood to hollow it out. With Akwa's and the monkeys' help, they carved out the inside with clamshells and oyster shells.

The next day he turned it over to shape the curved hull, then he flipped it back and resumed shaping the hollow inside the hull to make it float. And then they all joined in to sand the outside of the hull with shells and rocks so that it was nice and smooth. The finished canoe hull was about one metre wide, one metre deep and three metres long.

Helpful Monkeys

"Now we have to make an outrigger and attach it with bamboo poles," said Tahi-Akir.

The monkeys took them to a bamboo grove further along the island where they cut two long poles and one shorter pole with a machete that Zandra had provided. They dragged the bamboo poles slowly back to the beach and floated them back to the hull that waited for them further down the lagoon. The bamboo cross poles were about ten centimetres in diameter and a bit longer than three quarters of the length of the canoe. The outrigger was capped on the front end with a cone-shaped driftwood plug so they were watertight.

Then they fastened the boat and bamboo together with wooden and bamboo pegs.

"Now we need to lash it together," said Tahi-Akir. The resourceful monkeys found some hemp bushes which Akwa and Zandra fashioned into twisted ropes.

Then they put it all together. Tahi-Akir fashioned some paddles to steer the canoe.

After two weeks of work, the canoe was ready.

Chapter 11

Home

Journey home

When the outrigger canoe was finally finished, Tahi-Akir and Akwa said farewell to Shakir and Zandra. The monkeys gave them bananas for their journey home.

Together they paddled the canoe across the lagoon, escorted by playful dolphins.

They rowed towards the village on the other side of the calm lagoon in a light breeze, which was lovingly provided by Sedna. As they skimmed over the calm water, the Jade Sea Dragon appeared, making happy humming sounds, which was another good sign from the sea goddess.

When they arrived on the lagoon side of the village, they beached their canoe and walked up through a plantation of banana and mango trees, passed the path to the ancient caves, and towards the village.

Suddenly, someone challenged them. "Who are you? Where did you come from?" It was Kiwi, Akwa's best friend, who was picking mangoes from one of the trees.

"It's me. Akwa," she said excitedly. "I have returned from my journey to visit Zandra on the other side of the island. And I have found my father!" The two women happily embraced and jumped up and down together with joy.

"Oh! I am over the moon! It's so good to see you and feel you. I was worried something had happened to you – you left so many weeks ago! Now I know you are really here," said Kiwi, "and I am sure everyone else in the village will be overjoyed to hear the good news and see you both safely returned home." She welcomed Tahi-Akir with a big hug.

They all walked arm in arm toward the village.

Village Reunion

Arriving home, Akwa and Tahi-Akir had a joyful reunion with Moana and the other relieved villagers.

The men had mended their nets and rebuilt their boats, so there was plenty of fish from the fishermen, who had experienced calm seas and abundant fishing while Akwa had been away. They had also rebuilt their homes and the village.

There was a big feast and a dance that night, and Akwa shared her adventures. The storytelling went on for weeks.

Tahi's Teachings

Tahi-Akir told the villagers how he was lost at sea, and they were amazed by his story. He said that he was swept off the fishing boat by a big wave and hit his head. The monkeys found him washed up on the eastern shore. He also conveyed his experiences with Akwa's patience and her powerful healing energy.

Tahi-Akir spoke about Shakir and the wisdom of the shaman and his lessons. He advised them that he wanted to teach the rituals to the males in the village, and they were excited by the challenge.

He taught the men and initiated boys about many things: how to tune into and control powerful masculine energy and what a man's empowerment is all about. They explored how to use the energies and elements of the seven directions (North, East, West, South, Up, Down and Centre). He showed a select few how to be in control of and safely use the trance-state and how to assist confused spirits to find peace and pass on.

With teens and children, Tahi-Akir had fun when he showed them how to see and feel their auras and what different colours of auras meant. The astute ones also practised how to use the information to help and heal people. He gave instruction on the many ways to interpret prophetic dreams and visions. Of course, developing their intuition and leadership skills were also very valuable lessons.

For interested adults, there were advanced studies about the links between sexuality and spirituality. He also taught the advanced spiritual students how to use guided meditation, how to explore portals and go on inter-dimensional journeys, using rituals and proper guidelines.

We are all Sea Players

Akwa told her family and friends about her interactions with Sedna the Sea Goddess and Pela the Mountain Goddess.

She told them about the lagoon and the dolphins and that it was safe to swim and sail there now. She gave them all the details of her journey, the Jade Sea Dragon, Shakir the shaman and the helpful, playful monkeys. The elders listened, amazed, when she explained about Pela and about how she had patiently healed Tahi-Akir. The villagers all listened eagerly, fascinated by her courage and adventures.

Akwa showed them the shells she had gathered from the other side of the island and taught the women how to make shell flutes. She told them that they were all Sea Players. Together, they made up tunes to play to show love, gratitude and appreciation to the sea goddess, and they sang and played every day at the Sea Temple.

The Yellow Boat

When prompted, Moana told Akwa more details about the story of her beginnings on the island. She confirmed that Akwa was found in a strange, yellow metal boat named

Artiye. Akwa resolved to find this boat to look at it, because she was curious to know about her heritage.

"Who would know where this strange boat is stored?" asked Akwa curiously.

"I cannot say, however you can ask the village elders when you see them tomorrow, and they will probably be able to tell you. When you tell them what Zandra told you…" said Moana mysteriously.

***

The next day, Akwa and Moana visited the village elders. The gathered in the elder's cave with the runes and symbols, and Akwa realised they were now very familiar. They were the very same symbols as in Zandra's dwelling. *So, Zandra was once an elder here, too,* thought Akwa.

Akwa told them what Zandra had explained to her about her origins in the stars, her yellow pod boat and the next phase of her quest. She also revealed her translation crystal and the healing gossamer, explaining their uses.

"Zandra told me about the ancient people who came from the stars. They lived on this island and built the tunnels and the caverns," said Akwa. "She also said that there are instructions for me in my yellow pod boat. It came from my starship, which could be stored in the Royal Caves. With your permission, I would like to see it."

The elders were indignant. "We cannot take you to the Royal Caves until you are initiated."

"When can I be initiated?" asked Akwa.

"When you are sixteen," one replied authoritatively.

"Akwa has been away, and more than six moons have passed since she celebrated her 'day of birth' which was actually the day she was found on the beach," said Moana, "so I respectfully submit that she qualifies to be initiated."

"We will have to vote on this unusual situation in the village council meeting," said one of the elders.

Chapter 12

Dreams

Learning and Healing

From her initial journey across Bula Island, Akwa learned about persistence, endurance, survival, and how to tune in to her intuition and follow her instincts. By finding out the big picture for her life, it reawakened her urge to continue learning and teaching, to fulfil her life purpose to explore, heal, and give and receive love, following the destiny of her life.

Akwa did a lot of healing when she returned to the village. Using special blessed water from the mountain streams, she washed away pain and healed with the coloured water and native herbs as Zandra had shown her. She found that gossamer from spider webs worked just as well as that from the Jade Sea

Dragon to sanitise and heal open wounds, which the fishermen often got from coral cuts.

She taught the girls and women about their "Wise Woman Within " and the moon cycles. She explained about the five elements: water, wood, fire, metal and earth.

Akwa also taught the villagers about Spiritual Cleansing. She first asked them to rub their hands together, to feel their aura or spiritual energy. "I have used this when I was upset, sad, depressed, angry, fearful or negative. I've also used it when something unexpected happens, or to increase my energy when I feel lazy, or to calm myself when I feel too much 'busy-ness' or overwhelmed. Let me know tomorrow what you use it for during the rest of today and tonight."

The next day, she asked them how they used Spiritual Cleansing. "My little sister annoyed me," said Kiwi, "so I used it to calm myself, and I also taught her how to do it!"

"I used it when the waves got big and I was scared," said a young fisherman.

Kriti said that she was still feeling sad because her grandmother died many moons ago and she missed her, so she used the Spiritual Cleansing to feel at peace.

***

Every day, Akwa played her shell flute to the sea, with aloha love. The women played and sang with her. Akwa listened to the sea goddess' reply, for only she could hear it, with the aid of the red coral jewel. Sedna was very happy!

When the Sea Traders came to the island, Akwa translated their words using her red coral jewel translator. They told her exciting stories of other places in the world, and Akwa dreamed of travelling away with the Sea Traders.

***

Shakir and Zandra came and visited the village every month and taught the young men and women about many more fascinating things, answering their numerous questions with their extensive wisdom.

Akwa visited Zandra every year on the day of the anniversary of the Full Moon tsunami which started her journey.

Akwa's Dreams

Akwa told Zandra of recurring dreams that she had been having. She often remembered in her dreams that she was flying above a big land which had no sea, no ocean. She also had dreams about flying to the moon. And a red-haired Moon Goddess…

Eventually Akwa was initiated and taken to the Royal Caves where her yellow metal pod boat had been stored and preserved. It was covered with a special cover to stop it rusting from the sea air, and it was made of a different metal to any the villagers had ever seen before.

Akwa often sat in it and tried to find out how to control it, but it was a mystery to her.

One day, she touched the inside underneath the window and a part of the wall slid away. There were buttons and dials underneath, and she pressed a glowing triangle button. Akwa jumped up when a strange voice started talking. She put her translator jewel in her ear and listened. The voice described a planet called Hadar and a long journey through the stars. The purpose of the journey was to study an interesting planet they had been watching from their starships.

She listened, fascinated, to the strange, disembodied voice. She discovered, by trial and error, that she could stop it with the square symbol button. She sat there for a long time, feeling excited and scared at the same time. The past and the future were coming together.

Every day she sat in her starship and listened to the stories of another planet, another life. It was fascinating. And then she pressed the big round button, and the starship began to vibrate…

To be continued …

Glossary

Akwa (also spelled Aqua) means The Great One or The Essential One. Kwa or Qua means Essential One or Great One. (Nigerian). In this story, Akwa is the Chosen One.

Akir is an Arabic name for a male, and it means "Intelligent, Anchor, Bright".

Bard is a storyteller. The role of the storyteller on Bula Island was to entertain and educate. A bard performed the functions of storyteller, historian, ambassador, and more.

A good storyteller will typically identify their two most salient points and bookend their story with them — they will open with an exciting anecdote to grab the audience's attention, and then they will make sure the last thing they say is something that can resonate with the audience long after the story is over.

A **Blood moon** is when Earth's moon is in a total lunar eclipse, and the usually milky moon in the sky looks as if it is coloured red or ruddy-brown.

Gaia is the Greek goddess of Earth, mother of all life; similar to the Roman Terra Mater (Mother Earth); or the Andean Pachamama.

Gossamer is spider web. Did you know that spider web is excellent for sealing wounds? It has been used for this purpose by many people. The reason for its healing powers is because it is soft and strong and also it can provide protection from bacterial infection.

Leilani means "royal child" or "heavenly flowers" (from Hawaiian "*lei*" to mean flowers/child and "*lani*" which means sky/heaven/royal).

Moana means ocean, or sea. This beautiful gender-neutral name is a favourite in many

Polynesian places like Tahiti, Samoa and New Zealand. It has a gentle melodious sound that's pronounced "moh-AH-nah" and means "ocean, sea, wide expanse of water" in most Polynesian languages.

A **Moon Calendar** is a handy way to successfully plant crops and plan fishing. The benefits of gardening by the moon haves been known for thousands of years. Just as the moon influences the rise and fall of the tides, plants (and people), which have a high water content, are also influenced by the moon's phases. Bula Island villagers used the moon's phases and lunar cycles to know the right time to plant, when to fertilise and when to cultivate their crops and fruit trees.

Namaste is a common, respectful greeting in many cultures. "*Nama* means bow; *as* means I; and *te* means you," so therefore, namaste literally means 'bow me you' or 'I bow to you.'

Occiput refers to the back of the head. It is not a synonym for the occipital bone. The occipital bone is also known as "C0" because it joins the skull to the first cervical vertebra or C1, forming the atlanto-occipital joint.

Pela or Pele is the Hawaiian goddess of fire and volcanoes, and she helps to create and destroy islands. She is also known as Pelahonuamea – "She who shapes the sacred land."

Piupiu is a skirt-like garment made of flax strands that hang from a belt. They are worn by women and men in New Zealand on special occasions. When the wearer moves or dances, the strands sway to and fro. Native New Zealanders use a traditional method using flax leaves to make *piupiu*.

Poi is a Maori word for "ball on a cord". Indigenous Maori people in New Zealand traditionally used one or two to increase their flexibility and strength in their hands and arms, and also to improve coordination.

Red coral is an especially popular and highly sought-after gemstone due to its deep red colour and shine. Because coral takes millions of years to form, coral gemstones are especially rare and very valuable.

Runes are symbols from ancient Germanic systems of runic alphabets. Although the runes – often made by sticks or carved onto stone, wood, bone and metal – represented letters, they were ideographic or pictographic symbols of some cosmological principle or power (like emojis). To use the runic language meant invoking the force for which it stood. The word *rune* means to carve or to cut, and it comes from the word *runo*, meaning letter and mystery.

Sea Traders are persons who engage in trade by moving or selling goods on the seas and they engage in foreign or coastal trade.

Sedna comes from the Inuktitut or Inuit people in northern Canada. Called Sanna, or Sidne, she is the goddess of the sea and marine animals in Inuit mythology, also known as the Mother of the Sea or Mistress of the Sea.

Shakir is a male Arabic name which means "grateful", "thankful". Al-Shakir (Ash-Shakir) "the All-Thankful" is an attribute of Allah.

A **Shaman** is a person regarded as having access to, and influence in, the world of good and evil spirits, especially among some peoples of northern Asia and North America. Typically, shamans enter a trance state during a ritual, and practise divination and healing.

Another definition of a shaman is a person believed to achieve various powers through trance or ecstatic religious experience. Although a shaman's talents vary from one culture to the next, they are typically thought to have the ability to heal the sick, communicate with the otherworld, and escort the souls of the dead to that otherworld.

Sometimes shamans are "chosen" by their different attitudes to the world and life, and they can inherit or take on promising apprentices to train. A shaman is literally "one who knows." Shamans include women, men, and transgender individuals of every age from middle childhood onward.

Tahi is a name which comes from Polynesia. The meaning of Tahi is "one who lives by the sea". Tahi also means number one in Maori language

Third Eye is a mystical invisible eye that is in the centre of your forehead, above your nose. It symbolises psychic perception beyond ordinary sight.

Trolls are large, magical beasts who are very strong and sometimes slow to understand. A troll is a supernatural being in Norse mythology and Scandinavian folklore. In Old Norse sources, trolls were said to dwell in isolated rocks, mountains or caves, living together in small family units and were rarely helpful to human beings.

Zandra means "helper and defender of mankind". It is a short form of Alexandra.

The Ancient Runes and their Meanings

	Name	Possible Meanings	Moana's Interpretation
1	Nadh	Distress, grace, survival	Lost
2	Tyr	Man, leadership, honour, authority	Man
3	Ka	Boat, chew, pine, daring, bold, nothing	At sea.
4	Logr	Sea, liquid, moisture, water, emotions, the unknown dreams	Sea Goddess
5	Hagal	Destructive forces, uncontrolled forces	Anger
6	W	Big waves	Huge waves
7	Kyn	Nature, reproductive power, generous	Gigantic waves

	Name	Possible Meanings	Moana's Interpretation
8	Ur	Life after death, storm, original, eternity, procreation	A storm, destruction
9	Perth	Fruitful tree, initiation, game, things unexplained, something hidden	Fruit on a tree survives for people to eat
10	Yr	Wrong or mistaken, error, wrath, iris, bow, rainbow, anger	Be open to changing your interpretation
11	Bar	Woman, birth, goddess, growth	A woman with gifts, a journey to consult the goddess and spirit guides
12	Raidho	Journey, Ride,	A big journey
13	Gibor	Gift, giver, god, spirit guides	Guidance, help and support from spirit guides, gods and goddesses

How Akwa and the Sea Goddess was created

On 19 June 2021 I woke up in the middle of the night (which is unusual for me) and started writing about a very clear vision I had in a dream that I wanted to capture. One hour and eleven handwritten pages later, I had the entire first draft of *The Sea Players*. When I re-read it the next day, I liked the story. It follows the classic 'hero's journey' genre. I told a few friends about it, gave them copies to read, and they encouraged me to expand on it and publish it. This is how *Akwa and the Sea Goddess* was born!

As an artist, I have also created my own illustrations for this book, which will be available soon as a colouring book.

After many edits and additions, suggestions from friends who have read it, many prompts from emails, pictures and other 'signs' that I need to write this book and publish it, here it is!

Acknowledgements

A huge amount of gratitude to Ann Baker and Lisa Fabry for the proofreading and editing suggestions. Thanks to Jill Clarke and Mia Borodacz for their proofreading, support and inspiration.

Thanks to my Canadian friend Mia for telling me the story about Sedna, the Inuit Sea Goddess, which I didn't know about when I originally wrote this story.

Also I would like to thank 11 year old Mia Baker for her invaluable feedback as a young adult.

Thank you to Emily Gowor for her inspiration, feedback and technical support about publishing and editing.

To my wonderful editor, Dominic Gilmour, many thanks for your editing, wonderful plot suggestions and other improvements.

Also my gratitude to SusansArt for her visualization and creation of the beautiful cover design and Bula Island illustration.

I'm grateful to Chandrashekhar Yadav for his typesetting skills and patience.

About the Author

Ally Thomas is an author, artist, trainer, Personal Organiser, Transformational Relationship Consultant, Teacher and Healer.

She was born in New Zealand and now lives happily in Adelaide, Australia and loves living on and visiting islands of all shapes and sizes. Since 2008 she has run her own massage and healing business. She enjoys writing educational, fun and inspirational books about love and relationships.

She has been an artist since 2017 and loves drawing with watercolour pencils and painting with acrylic paints.

Ally's websites are www.allythomas.com.au and
www.allyacupressure.com.au.

She is also on Facebook and Instagram.

9 780099 462284 6